A LAURA MARLIN MYSTERY

THE MIDNIGHT PICNIC

THE MIDNIGHT PICNIC

Lauren St John

Illustrated by David Dean

Children's Books

First published in Great Britain in 2014
by Orion Children's Books
a division of the Orion Publishing Group Ltd
Orion House
5 Upper St Martin's Lane
London WC2H 9EA

1 3 5 7 9 10 8 6 4 2

The Orion Publishing Group's policy is to use papers that
are natural, renewable and recyclable products and made
from wood grown in sustainable forests. The logging and
manufacturing processes are expected to conform to the
environmental regulations of the country of origin.

A catalogue record for this book is available
from the British Library

Printed in Great Britain by Clays Ltd, St Ives plc

ISBN 978 1 4440 1228 6

www.laurenstjohn.com
www.orionbooks.co.uk

For Georgie Adams,
With thanks for NOT getting
me lost on Bodmin Moor

ONE

'Have a great time. Be good and be careful,' said Calvin Redfern, handing his niece her backpack and sleeping bag as she boarded the St Ives school bus with her three-legged Siberian husky, Skye.

Laura Marlin hopped up the steps and turned to give him a smile and a wave.

'It's only a picnic, Uncle Calvin, and we're only going an hour or so up the road, not to St Petersburg or the Caribbean or anywhere else exotic. We have three teachers supervising our every move. What could possibly go wrong?'

He folded his arms across his broad chest and shook his head. 'Laura Marlin, I can't believe you just said that! You don't exactly have the best track record when it comes to *not* getting into trouble, you know. And this is no ordinary picnic. It's at night. Why on earth is it at night?'

His words were drowned out as the bus roared to life. 'Don't worry,' Laura called. 'Tariq and Skye are with me. They'll keep me safe.'

'That,' Calvin Redfern remarked drily,

'is what you told me the last time – right before you were kidnapped. And the time before that when you almost rode off a cliff on a horse. And the time before that when you were nearly incinerated by–'

He stopped. The bus door had hissed closed and it was obvious from the grin on Laura's face as she went to sit beside Tariq Ali, the Bengali boy who was her best friend, that she'd missed most of what her uncle had said. Or had heard but chosen to ignore him. But she did have a point. It *was* only a school trip and Tariq and Skye *were* with her. He'd have preferred it if it was an afternoon picnic rather than a sleepover on Bodmin Moor, but at least she would be relatively close to home. In an emergency, he could race out to get her.

The other thing he needed to remind himself was that the trip was a special treat for a select group of prize-winning Year 6's, of whom Laura was one. He should be proud. He *was* proud.

As Laura had said, what could possibly go wrong?

'I still can't believe that Mr Gillbert chose my idea,' said Camilla Lawson with a flick of her blonde hair. 'It is a great one but with nineteen other names in the pot I wasn't expecting mine to be chosen. Not that I'm boasting. You don't have to worry that the Student of the Year Award is going to go to my head. I'll still be the same old Camilla.'

'You mean, the one with an ego the size of a hot-air balloon?' muttered Rainbow Brown under her breath. 'That's something to look forward to.'

Behind her, Laura stifled a giggle.

'What was that?' demanded Camilla.

Laura buried her face in Skye's fur and said nothing. She could feel Tariq shaking with silent laughter beside her. Camilla and Rainbow were opposites and they were always taking swipes at one another. Camilla's father was a hedge-fund manager, which had nothing to do with managing hedges and everything to do with making millions. He worked in London during the week and returned to the family's beachfront mansion at weekends.

Rainbow's parents, on the other hand,

were hippies who wore lots of purple and lived in a motor-home on a plot of land near Carbis Bay. They had three children, six chickens, two goats, four dogs and a cat and grew all their own food.

'I was *saying*,' continued Rainbow Brown, 'that the whole point of this trip is that the wish lists of all of the award winners have been mixed into one. You might have come up with the midnight feast idea, but it was Laura who wanted to go on a picnic and Tariq who asked to go camping. It's Katie's birthday so she's having a special cake. Jamie got to be involved with choosing the food and I asked if we could go to Bodmin Moor. Everyone on this bus has played a part in making today special.'

'I really don't understand your point,'

said Camilla. 'I wished for a midnight feast and that's what we're having . . .'

Rainbow mimed banging her head on the back of Laura and Tariq's seat. Her pigtails swung back and forth. 'If I haven't pushed Camilla into a bog before the night is through, it'll be a total miracle,' she whispered to them.

'What I'd like to know is why Laura gets to bring Skye when none of us are allowed to bring our dogs,' whined Adam Sears. 'How is that fair?'

'Yes, and I had to leave Hamish, my hamster,' sighed Katie. 'He's only small. What difference would it have made if he was in my bag?'

'There are two excellent reasons why Skye has been allowed to come and Dinky,

Hamish and all the other dogs, goats and guinea pigs in St Ives have not,' said Miss Creswell, overhearing them. 'As you are perfectly well aware, Skye is the star of a film coming out later this year and that makes him something of a special case. I'm sure you'll remember that it was Laura's essay about her adventures with Tariq and Skye on the film set in Russia that won her the school essay prize.'

'And what's the other?' asked Adam. 'You said there were two reasons.'

Miss Creswell dabbed at her nose with a tissue. Her hay fever was playing up. 'The other is that we want a peaceful, fun night on the moors, not one full of fighting dogs or cats eating hamsters. You're forgetting that today is about rewarding you for your hard work during the term. It's supposed to be a treat. With all this chattering, you're missing the scenery. Look out of the window and take in the view.'

The bus immediately fell silent. Twenty faces were glued to the glass as they left behind the peacock blue of the sea that hugged St Ives, the pretty Cornish town that had been Laura's home for the past seven months. Before she'd discovered that she had an uncle who was alive and willing to adopt her, she'd spent eleven deathly dull years at Sylvan Meadows, an orphanage in a cold, grey town in the North. Now she lived with Calvin Redfern, a former detective, in his big rambling house overlooking golden Porthmeor Beach.

But it wasn't just St Ives that was

responsible for Laura's happiness. It was at least partly the fact that, since leaving Sylvan Meadows, she'd had a succession of hair-raising adventures. Some girls might have been alarmed by the rate at which death and disaster routinely confronted them, but not Laura. She dreamed of being a great detective like her uncle when she was older and, as far as she was concerned, the more mysteries she had to practise on now, the better she'd be in the future.

'Never a dull moment,' she murmured.

'Oh, there probably will be a couple,' said Tariq with a grin. He knew his best friend as well as he knew himself. She was drawn to intrigue like a bee to honey. 'I mean, we're on a school trip. It'll be fun, but you can forget about having adventures. Mr Gillbert's already given us five lectures about health and safety on the moors and we'll have four people watching to see that we obey every rule – three teachers and Camilla.'

Laura giggled. 'Except that Camilla is stricter than all of the teachers put together. How did we get so lucky?'

'What was that?' said Camilla, looking up from the school yearbook, which had a cover photo of her beaming with the Student of the Year trophy.

'Nothing,' said Laura. 'I was only saying that we're fortunate to have so many people taking care of us this evening.'

'Yes, you are,' Camilla said smugly. 'Between us, Mr Gillbert, Miss Creswell,

Mrs Archer and I have thought of everything. Nothing could possibly go wrong.'

TWO

The first thing they noticed as they approached Bodmin Moor was that it had its own micro-climate. St Ives had been bathed in sunshine, but in North Cornwall billowing pillars of clouds rose from behind the hillsides and tree-tops as if the horizon was smoking. The lanes narrowed too. As the bus scraped through ever-decreasing tunnels of green, Laura sucked in her stomach as if that would somehow make the bus smaller.

Late afternoon they stopped at Golitha Falls, a series of mini waterfalls that flowed through an ancient beech forest. Mr Gillbert laid rugs beside the lacy swirl of water while Mrs Archer dispensed iced lemonade. Since midnight was still six hours away, Katie's birthday cake was brought out in case anyone was hungry. Laura gave Skye a bone so that he didn't feel left out. He took it from her delicately and carried it to a quiet spot under a tree. As she joined in the chorus of 'Happy Birthday', Laura looked around and realised that everyone was having a great time, including the twins, Phillip and Amy, who claimed to hate nature.

'Make a wish, Katie,' urged Miss Creswell, and Katie quickly closed her eyes. When she opened them again she wore a secretive smile.

'What did you wish for?' Camilla wanted to know.

'If she tells you it won't come true,' said Adam, 'and that would be unfortunate if she's wished that you'd mind your own business and vanish into the mists of Bodmin Moor or something.'

'Now, now, Adam, there's no need to be like that,' Miss Creswell scolded, pushing her over-sized glasses firmly into place. She was a slender young teacher with an anxious manner and a kind heart.

'Apologise at once. Camilla has worked very hard to make this trip a success for everyone.'

'I was only joking,' said Adam. 'Anyway, there isn't any mist . . .' But he grudgingly added a 'sorry'.

With only a couple of kilometres to go until they reached Bodmin, butterflies began to skitter in Laura's stomach. Ever since she'd first heard about the moor, she'd longed to visit it. Even the name sounded mysterious.

For over six thousand years, humans had been coming to this wild place and yet even though they'd mined it, farmed it and fought battles on it, the landscape remained as untamed as ever. Before the trip, the teachers had drummed into the children that it was an area that could be really dangerous. There were bogs and Neolithic burial chambers and pits from the days when tin and copper was mined, and 'foxholes', hideouts that had been used by soldiers in the Second World War.

'Not so long ago this area was popular with smugglers,' Mr Gillbert had told them. 'Another thing you have to watch out for is sudden changes in weather. Bodmin is 208 kilometres square. That's a lot of wilderness to lose yourself in if a fog descends. And, of course, there's the legendary Beast of Bodmin – a black cat the size of a panther that is said to stalk the moors. You wouldn't want to come face to face with that.'

The brakes squealed, making Laura

jump. The bus was pulling into a car park. Before them stretched the moors, a purple carpet of heather mixed with bracken and yellow gorse flowers. Clouds the height of sky-scrapers lumbered at ground level, as if they were too swollen with raindrops to remain in the heavens.

As the bus doors opened, Skye leapt out before Laura could grab him, and raced round excitedly.

'If there are any rabbits about, they'd be better off hiding in their burrows until Skye leaves town,' Tariq teased as they followed him.

'Skye won't touch the rabbits,' Laura said loyally but not very confidently. 'He'll be too busy guarding us from the Beast of Bodmin.'

She was joking, but Kayla, a girl with long black hair and strange violet eyes, gave her a serious stare. 'You shouldn't say things like that in places like this. Don't you know that when you enter them you're crossing from one world to another? Ghosts walk these moors. None of the ordinary rules apply.'

'Oh, they'll be applied all right,' said Mrs Archer sternly. 'Have no fear about that. Now gather your belongings and let's get moving. We have tents to put up.'

THREE

Putting up the tents was a comical exercise in the wind, especially since the boys made a worse job of it than the girls. This was because the girls were assisted by Mr Gillbert, who, it turned out, went camping nearly every weekend and was an expert. It was also because the boys were hampered by Skye, who saw every rope as a snake and an excuse for a game of tug of war.

But at last the tents were up. Their campsite was a garden on the edge of the moor belonging to friends of one of the teachers. The family was away on holiday but had left the keys to a one-room cottage that lay beyond their orchard so the children could use the shower and toilet. Miss Creswell, who had numerous allergies, was going to sleep in the bedroom.

'Everyone else will be at one with nature,' Mrs Archer informed them. 'It'll be both character-building and fun.'

'Whenever teachers say that something is character-building, they usually mean it is the opposite of fun,' Laura commented to Tariq.

With the exception of the twins, who were concerned about 'bugs and other biting things', everyone was keen to explore. Only five minutes' walk from the house was one of Bodmin's most iconic landmarks, a curious ring of standing stones known as the Hurlers. Legend said that when a group of villagers played the Cornish game of hurling on a Sunday instead of going to church, Saint Cleer was so angry that he turned them to stone.

It was a story that would have been hard to believe if they'd been anywhere else, but out on the lonely moor it was eerily imaginable. Laura laid a hand on one of the tall stones and was sure she felt an energy radiating from it. The granite seemed to throb with some unseen life. But, of course, that was nonsense. The story of the Hurlers was a myth like so many others on Bodmin Moor.

'It's spooky,' Amy said with a shudder. 'Bodmin is not at all like it looks in the tourist brochures, with cool balancing rocks and otters paddling in streams. We could be on the moon, especially since Mrs Archer banned us from bringing our phones. What happens if there's an emergency?'

'It is quite isolated but I love it,' said Tariq. He adored nature. 'And there's nothing to worry about really. The teachers have their phones so they can easily ring for help if they need to.'

'Yes, we can,' said Mr Gillbert, coming up behind them. 'But rest assured, Amy, no help will be needed.' He paused as Miss Creswell had another sneezing fit. She was allergic to both pollen and Skye, and her hay-fever medicine had so far failed to work. 'Unless,' he added, 'it's an emergency dash for extra tissues. Amy, I would like to remind you that we are here for a rather special picnic. It's supposed to be a treat to reward you for your hard work. I hope you'll relax and enjoy yourself. We have a lovely evening planned for you all.'

No sooner had he spoken than the early evening sun burst through the clouds and lent a magical glow to the wildflowers and rolling hills. The brick towers that had been built during Cornwall's mining days were etched against the sky like castles and a couple of hawks twisted overhead.

Mr Gillbert, a keen birdwatcher, identified them as buzzards, but only Tariq and Laura were interested. Far more fascinating to most were the strange tales that were as much a part of Bodmin as the unseen creatures that rustled and scattered as they explored the moor.

In the distance, they could see the Cheesewring, another famous Bodmin landmark. Immense flat boulders formed a crooked tower nearly ten metres high. In defiance of gravity, the biggest rocks balanced on the smallest ones at impossible angles and on a downslope. It was hardly surprising that the locals had once believed that the structure was the result of a battle between the giants and the saints.

The boys were desperate to go there at once and climb on it but Laura was content to survey the bleak expanse of moorland. The sky to the north had turned a dark grape colour and the temperature had dropped sharply. She hoped it wasn't going to rain on their picnic.

'Please, Mr Gillbert, tell us another story,' begged Phillip, who seemed to have forgotten his dislike of the great outdoors.

The teacher was pleased by his interest. 'I have to say that some of the tales about Bodmin send chills up my spine. Take the Cheesewring rocks, for example. There are those who claim that if you visit the quarry at midnight and hear a cock crow, the top stone will revolve several times.'

'Oh, that's super cool,' cried Adam. 'I'm going to do that.'

'I'll come too,' said Nico, a dark-haired Italian boy with a gleam in his eye.

'I think not,' said Mr Gillbert. 'We are returning to our garden campsite and that is where we will remain until the bus arrives to take us home to St Ives at 10 a.m. tomorrow. Besides, at midnight you will be too busy enjoying your picnic to have any thoughts of wandering the moors.'

He glanced at the sky. 'As I've told you, the weather on Bodmin can change in moments. I think I just felt a drop of rain, let's hurry back. Believe me, Adam, I understand the lure of Bodmin, but one foolish mistake can turn deadly.'

FOUR

With so many dangers lurking on Bodmin Moor, it was ironic that Amy fell down the steps of the cottage at around 9.30 p.m. She let out a piercing scream. At the time, her classmates and the three teachers were watching *The Hound of the Baskervilles* on an outdoor screen and for a minute everyone thought her cry was part of the plot. Tariq reacted first. He rushed to her side, followed by Skye, Phillip and everyone else.

It was obvious that Amy had broken her wrist. It hung limply at an unnatural angle and began to swell immediately.

'Of all the bad luck!' cried Mr Gillbert. 'I can't believe it. We walk the moors safely and it ends in tears because of a concrete step.'

At that, Amy sobbed even harder. But all the tears in the world didn't alter the fact that, for her, the picnic was over. Within minutes, she was wrapped in a blanket and being whisked in the direction of the Royal Cornwall Hospital by Mrs Archer, who had come to Bodmin in her own car. With them were Mr Gillbert and Phillip, who was doing his best to hide his disappointment.

'We'll be back as soon as we can,' Mr Gillbert had called, 'but we have to drive miles to Truro so we may be some time. Until then, Miss Creswell and Camilla are in charge.'

Camilla's head swelled visibly at this news, while Miss Creswell was more like an anxious hen (one allergic to pollen and dogs) than ever.

'Oh, dear,' she said, dabbing at her scarlet nose. 'I hope we don't have any more incidents or accidents. I'm not much use to anyone in this condition.'

'I have a couple of hay-fever tablets if you'd like them,' said Camilla. 'My dad gave them to me in case I was allergic to the moor, but I've been perfectly fine, as usual. My mum says that I'm the healthiest person she knows.'

Behind her, Rainbow Brown groaned and performed a pantomime of throttling Camilla.

'Are you sure?' said the teacher, who had her back to Rainbow and didn't notice. 'That would be wonderful if you can spare them.'

After some discussion it was agreed that the film should resume and that they should try to have the best possible evening in Amy's honour. The projector purred and soon Sherlock Holmes was striding across Dartmoor in pursuit of a savage hound.

Laura's detective idol was Matt Walker, fictional hero of her favourite novels, but Sherlock Holmes' methods of deduction never failed to dazzle her, so as far as she was concerned the evening was complete even before the promised picnic. She lay on the grass using Skye as a pillow and enjoyed every moment of the film, even the scary bits.

Miss Creswell, who'd been cured of her hay fever by Camilla's pills, was all smiles as she handed out bowls of popcorn and fizzy drinks and the little garden campsite was quite festive by the time the film ended.

It was 11 p.m. when Tariq and Adam lit the lanterns. They glowed between the tents and cast golden stripes of light across the picnic table, where the food was being set out by Laura and Kayla. The barbecue had reached the perfect heat and Jamie was grilling beef and veggie burgers. There was also chargrilled sweetcorn and jacket potatoes cooked in the coals.

'I don't think that we need to wait for midnight to start our picnic,' said Miss Creswell, stifling a yawn and triggering yawns in several others. 'As long as we're eating at midnight, that's all that matters. We don't want to be too hungry and tired to enjoy it.'

Her suggestion was met with enthusiastic agreement. They each took a paper plate and formed an eager queue. Jamie, who had ambitions to follow in the footsteps of his chef hero and namesake, Jamie Oliver, had chosen the food. Everyone agreed that he'd done an incredible job. Along with the burgers and chips, there were slices of honey-roasted ham, salads, soft white rolls, strawberries and clotted cream and a mountain of chocolate brownies and homemade honeycomb ice-cream.

Laura gave Skye his own special plate of ham and chopped burger and he gobbled it up happily. Then he lay under an apple tree cleaning his paws and licking his lips until, quite suddenly, he went to sleep.

'Too much excitement,' said Tariq with a smile.

Laura felt as if she could easily do the same thing. Despite Amy's accident, it had turned into a lovely evening and the yummy food and peaceful glow of the lanterns made her feel like curling up in her tent and having a nap. Her eyelids fluttered closed. She snapped them open again. Miss Creswell was disappearing into the cottage.

Laura looked over at Skye. His head was up and he was gazing intently in the direction of the moors, which were screened by the orchard and a couple of big trees. She thought she heard the snarl of a wild animal, but before she could be sure Adam clicked on his iPod and music began to play.

'Is it just me or is it very smoky in the garden?' she asked Tariq.

Jamie checked the little gas stove. 'Shouldn't be. I've turned everything off.'

Kayla put down her brownie and got to her feet. 'It's not smoke, silly, it's fog.'

'Don't be daft,' said Adam with a laugh, but he got up and rushed to the garden gate, followed by everyone else.

They were met with an eerie sight. Fog so dense that they could barely see across the gravel road swirled thickly over the moor, blotting out everything except the area immediately in front of them.

'Wow,' breathed Adam. 'That's the coolest thing I've ever seen.'

He crossed the road and stood on the grass opposite. Fingers of fog wrapped themselves around him, giving him the appearance of a ghost. 'Now you see me,' he laughed. 'Now you don't.' He stepped back and immediately vanished.

'Adam,' said Kayla. 'Don't mess around. You wouldn't believe how easy it is to get lost when it's like this.'

Silence.

'Adam?' called Camilla. 'Adam, that's not funny! I'm going to report you to Mr Gillbert when he gets back.' There was no answer. After a minute she tried again, this time more kindly. 'Adam, are you okay?'

'He's kidding around,' said Jamie. 'Let's go and have a cup of hot chocolate. He'll soon be back.'

They were only halfway to the food table when they heard footsteps and Adam came running up, grinning. 'Fooled ya!'

Kayla rolled her eyes. 'The only fool is you. Anyone who goes out on the moors in fog like this is asking for trouble.'

Adam scowled. 'I'm here, aren't I?'

He flung himself down on a picnic rug. While Laura and Jamie made hot chocolate with marshmallows in it, the others joined him. Soon they were all sitting in a circle, mugs in hand, and even Adam was smiling. Mist floated through the trees, giving the garden a mystical feel. A lantern cast a warm glow.

Nico put down his mug and cast a cheeky glance at the black-haired girl. 'Hey, Kayla, I overheard you telling Laura that when you come to Bodmin you cross the line from one world to another. You said ghosts walked these moors. Know any good stories?'

She studied him with her violet eyes. 'A few. I know that there have been over sixty sightings of the giant black cat they call the Beast of Bodmin. There's also a couple of blurry photos. No one has been able to prove that it exists but no one has been able to disprove it either. But it is not the Beast I'm afraid of, it's Charlotte Dymond.'

Adam sat forward. 'Charlotte who?'

'She was found murdered, not far from here. Her boyfriend was later hanged at Bodmin Gaol for the crime. Since then, dozens of people have seen Charlotte's ghost walking the moors, dressed in a gown and silk bonnet.'

Laura shivered. Like the story of villagers turned to stone, it was not hard to believe, especially on such a creepy night.

'I think we've heard enough horrid

stories for one evening,' Camilla said crossly. 'Any more and we'll be having nightmares. Besides, we should be clearing up the picnic and going to bed.'

Adam laughed. 'Not likely. The fun is only just getting started.' He hooted like an owl in a scary movie. 'Whoo, whoo. No parents! No teachers!'

They all laughed and every head turned in the direction of the cottage. The building itself was hidden by mist, but the light from the bedroom shone strongly.

'Where is Miss Creswell anyway?' asked Katie. 'She's been gone for ages.'

'I expect she's waiting for news from the hospital,' said Camilla. 'She might be a while. Don't worry about her. Mr Gillbert said I'm next in charge. It's after midnight and I think it's time that everyone went to their tents.'

Rainbow laughed. 'Do you really? Well, I think I want to stay up and listen to ghost stories. If you don't want to join us, go away and leave us in peace.'

'Yes, take a walk in the fog or something,' said Adam. 'We're trying to enjoy ourselves and all you want to do is spoil everything.'

Camilla flushed with anger. She opened her mouth as if to say something, thought better of it and stalked off towards the cottage. Before she reached the path the mist had swallowed her.

Katie glared at Adam and Rainbow. 'That wasn't very nice of you, Adam. I know Camilla can be extremely annoying but she did work very hard to organise this whole picnic and she's been so looking forward to it.'

'Yes, she has,' agreed Laura.

'All right, all right, I'll go and say sorry,' Adam said huffily, 'but I'll give her a few minutes to cool down first.'

'I suppose I'd better come with you,' Rainbow said grudgingly, 'but first let's clear away the picnic. It'll make Camilla smile and she'll think that we do appreciate her after all. Everyone else can go to their tents if they're tired, or stay up telling ghost stories or playing games if they're not.'

Laura and Tariq looked at one another. They'd been up early that morning to swim before the tourists arrived at Porthmeor Beach. Now they were exhausted. So was

Skye, who kept yawning and looking at them as if to say, 'Are you *ever* going to bed?'

Laura laughed and gave him a cuddle. 'Come on, gorgeous. You can share my tent. I don't think Amy will be back tonight.'

Tariq, who'd been sharing with Phillip, was on his own too. His tent was next door to Laura's. They found a way to pin back the flaps of both so that they could lie in their sleeping bags and chat before they drifted off. But once she was tucked up and cosy, with Skye lying on her feet, all Laura could manage was a mumbled, 'Hope the Beast of Bodmin doesn't get us.'

Tariq laughed. Moments later, both were sound asleep. Only Skye stayed alert, one ear cocked, watching and waiting. He was tired but the fog had unsettled him. If something was lurking on the invisible moors, he wanted to be ready for it.

FIVE

In the dream a panther was pursuing Laura. The dark jungle was impenetrable and she couldn't see it, but she'd heard it roar and the savagery in the sound had reduced her to a trembling wreck.

The roar came again, cutting through the layers of sleep. Laura bolted upright, knocking over her bottle of water. The front entrance of the tent was zipped shut but Skye had his nose pressed to the air vent. His hackles were up. He gave a low growl that started deep in his chest and built steadily.

Laura reached for his collar. He whined and lay down but almost immediately he was up again. The roar came again and this time it was closer. Laura had to clap a hand over her mouth to stop herself screaming. Surely she was still trapped in a nightmare? Surely she hadn't just heard the Beast of Bodmin?

Her hand closed over her torch.

'Laura!' Tariq poked his head through the flap. 'Laura, are you awake? What was that?'

Before she could answer, they heard footsteps. 'Laura and Tariq, wake up.' It was Adam's voice, panicky and fearful.

Laura looked into the fog. It was draped across the garden like a net curtain. 'What's going on?' said Tariq, emerging from his tent in his pyjamas and switching on his torch. In the harsh beam, Adam was a ghastly white. Behind him were Nico and Rainbow, her eyes swollen from crying.

Rainbow spoke first. 'It's Miss Creswell and Camilla. They've gone!'

Laura stared at her, not understanding. 'What do you mean gone? Gone where? Did the bus come back?'

'I mean, they've disappeared. Vanished into thin air.'

'The bus hasn't come back and neither have Mr Gillbert and Mrs Archer,' put in Adam.

'But that's impossible,' said Tariq. 'Miss Creswell would never go off and leave us on our own.'

'Of course she wouldn't,' agreed Rainbow. 'Why do you think we're so upset? We're convinced that something terrible has happened to them and it's our fault. Maybe Camilla stormed off in a rage and Miss Creswell ran after her and now they're both lost on the moors. Maybe the Beast of Bodmin – the black panther or whatever it's supposed to be – has got them. It sounds as if it's out hunting.'

Tears filled her eyes again. 'What if

they're already dead and *we're* responsible?'

'There *is* no Beast of Bodmin,' said Tariq, but even as he spoke another blood-curdling roar cut through the night.

Laura grabbed Skye's collar. She didn't believe that an escaped panther was stalking the moors any more than she believed in ghosts. But what other explanation was there?

A tent shook nearby and two girls burst out. 'The Beast is coming for us,' cried Katie. 'It's going to eat us alive. We'll be ripped apart and all my mum and dad will find is my bones.'

Adam snapped into life. 'Don't be silly, Katie,' he said with surprising gentleness. 'Somebody's playing a game, that's all. We're going to find out who it is and tell them off. Go back to sleep and don't worry about it. When you get up in the morning, we'll have breakfast and laugh about this.'

Katie looked disbelieving. 'Are you sure? Who would play such a horrible game? It sounds so real.'

'It does but it's not. Now go back to your tent and don't open the flap!'

When Katie and Sammi had gone, he turned to Laura. 'At school you have a reputation as a bit of a detective. We need your help. You've got to find Miss Creswell and Camilla.'

A fresh wave of adrenalin surged through Laura's veins. She lived to solve mysteries, but that didn't mean she wasn't sometimes afraid while she was doing it. Still, she didn't hesitate. She and Tariq dived into their tents, pulled on jeans, sweaters and boots and they were ready.

'The first question I have to ask is the most obvious one,' Laura said as they hurried towards the cottage. 'What makes you think they're missing?'

'See for yourself,' said Rainbow as they went up the steps. Inside was a bathroom, clearly empty, and a tiny living room piled with picnic supplies and the teachers' rucksacks and suitcases. Even before they reached the tiny bedroom, Laura could see that the bed hadn't been slept in. A mirror at the foot of it reflected the carefully ironed sheets, pillowcases and duvet and the bedside table.

Laura stood at the door and took in the

scene. 'You do realise that we have no proof that Camilla ever came in here?'

Rainbow frowned. 'That's true, but the last time we saw her she was heading in this direction and she's not in her tent or shed or anywhere in the garden. We've hunted. Where else would she be? Her bag is on the sofa there and her pyjamas and clean clothes are still folded and packed. Would you like to see it?'

Inside the pink sports bag was a pair of pyjamas, a stuffed bear, a change of clothes and Camilla's toothbrush and toothpaste. There was also an empty case for a notebook computer. After studying it for a moment, Laura returned it to the bag.

'This was on the bed,' said Nico, holding

up a phone. 'It's Miss Creswell's but the battery's dead.'

Laura examined it. 'Great. Now we can't call for help even if we want to.'

She glanced at her watch. It was 1.15 a.m. The temperature had dropped sharply. If Miss Creswell and Camilla really were on the moors, the cold alone could kill them.

She came to a decision. 'We need a compass and a long rope. Anyone seen either of those things?'

'I have a compass on my keyring,' said Tariq.

'And I saw a rope coiled up outside the shed,' said Adam.

'Good. Would you mind grabbing it? Meet us at the garden gate.'

Three minutes later Laura, Tariq, Adam,

Rainbow and Kayla, who'd been woken by the roars, were gazing out at the foggy moor.

'You're seriously asking us to risk our lives by walking blindly into the fog with a predator on the loose?' said Kayla. 'And what about the ghost of Charlotte Dymond? Can't we put Skye on the trail of Miss Creswell and Camilla?'

Laura smiled. 'Skye isn't a bloodhound, so I can't send him out to hunt for lost teachers and students, but don't panic, you definitely won't be risking your life. That's why I asked Adam to bring a rope.'

'A rope? A gun is what we need, or a cricket bat. Something to beat the creature off if it attacks.'

Laura ignored her. She took the rope

from Adam and had each of them hold a section of it. 'This way, we're all connected. We don't want to lose anyone else.'

'What happens next?' asked Rainbow.

'We wait until we hear that noise again. When we do, we'll walk towards the sound. Tariq, Skye and me will go first.'

'You're mad,' said Kayla, letting go of the rope. 'I'm not going to risk being eaten by some crazy animal for the sake of Camilla. I'm going back to my tent.'

Laura studied the other tense faces. 'Anyone else?'

Adam shook his head. 'We're in.'

The sound came again. It was part roar, part snarl and it was terrifyingly close. Laura swallowed. If she was wrong, she could be leading them all into disaster. She looked at Tariq. He was nervous, she could tell, but he was also determined.

'Let's go,' he said.

SIX

Skye sprang forward, dragging Laura with him. She had to fight to cling on to her bit of the rope. The fog was like a living thing. It blinded her and crept into her lungs as if it was the breath of the moor itself. In an instant, the campsite was invisible.

The Beast had gone quiet, but the

husky's ears were pricked. He moved forward so rapidly that the ragged line of children struggled to keep up with him. They were scratched by gorse and tripped and stumbled, the arc of their torchlight swinging wildly. But it was only for a short distance. When the Beast roared again, it was so close that Rainbow screamed.

Laura looked back at her. 'Watch Skye. He's not afraid so you don't have to be either.'

It was true. The husky had stopped and was whining softly at a gorse bush. Laura let go of the rope, bent down and picked up an iPad that was hidden beneath it. She handed it to Rainbow.

'There's your Beast. Not scary at all, unless you're alone on a campsite beside a moor full of secrets on a dark night.'

'I don't believe it,' cried Adam. He took it from her. It had been set up to replay a video of wild tigers an infinite number of times at maximum volume. 'This is Camilla's, isn't it? I remember this video from a project she did on endangered animals a few months ago. Do you really think she did this to get back at us?'

'Definitely,' said Rainbow.

Adam laughed. 'What an awesome practical joke. I wish I'd thought of it. Who knew that she had such a wicked sense of humour.'

His smile faded as it dawned on him what finding the iPad meant. 'This is bad news, isn't it? She could be anywhere.'

'My guess is that she was on her way to

see Miss Creswell when she had the idea to play the trick on you,' said Laura. 'She came out here thinking that she'd hide the iPad and go straight back to the camp and she got lost. It can happen in the blink of an eye. If we didn't have Tariq and his compass, we'd be lost too.'

Rainbow looked utterly miserable. 'Oh, it's no use. How are we going to find her when we can barely see our hands in front of our faces?'

'We could do a series of arcs around this spot,' suggested Tariq, 'moving outward like ripples in a pond.'

Laura nodded agreement. 'That's exactly what we should do. That way, if she's fallen and is unconscious, we won't miss her.'

It was easier said than done. The fog was

so dense it was like walking blindfolded. With every step they had to face their own fears. Nico was terrified of stepping on an adder in the dark; Rainbow was afraid of ghosts; Tariq was afraid of being kidnapped and ending up in the hands of the men who'd once tried to turn him into a slave; Adam was scared of spiders and murderers; and Laura was convinced she was about to fall down an old mine shaft.

But they were driven on by a greater fear – of doing nothing when Camilla and Miss Creswell were in danger. They at least had each other and that bonded them more and more strongly with each step.

In the end it was the best part of an hour and they were hoarse from shouting and close to giving up when they heard a faint cry.

'Camilla!' shouted Laura.

'Help me! HELP!'

Adam let go of the rope and started running.

'Adam, wait,' cried Rainbow. 'We don't want to lose you too.'

'Let him go,' said Nico. 'He feels bad that he upset her. Let him make it right.'

When the clouds of fog finally rolled back to reveal the pair, they were hugging. Camilla separated from Adam and came flying towards them, embracing them each in turn and giving Skye a cuddle too. She was totally unrecognisable. Her silken blonde hair was knotted in clumps and full of bits of grass and greenery. Mud and slime coated her clothes and face.

'Well, you got your wish, Rainbow,' she said, half sobbing, half laughing. 'I did fall in a bog. Luckily, it wasn't too deep and I managed to get out, but there were times when I wondered whether you and Adam had supernatural powers because everything you wished for came true.'

Tears of shame came into Rainbow's eyes. 'I'm so, so sorry. I don't know how I'll ever make it up to you.'

'Nor me,' Adam told her. 'I'm sorry too. We were coming to apologise when we found you were missing.'

Camilla smiled. 'There is one thing you can do for me. Help me sneak back into the campsite and shower before any of the teachers find out what's happened.'

Adam laughed. 'It's a deal.'

Rainbow clapped a hand to her mouth. 'Miss Creswell! We've forgotten all about her.'

Camilla stared at her in confusion. 'What do you mean? Where is she? Isn't she at the campsite taking care of everyone?'

'No, she isn't,' said Tariq. 'She's disappeared too. We were hoping she was with you.'

Camilla paled. 'I haven't seen her. When I went into the cottage the bedroom door was closed and I just grabbed my iPad and rushed out. But where could she have gone? She'd never have gone off without telling anyone.'

'I am certain that she has been

kidnapped,' Nico said darkly. 'In Italy, the Mafia do these things all the time. Soon we will receive a ransom note.'

Tariq and Laura stole a glance at one another. Thanks to the exploits of the notorious Straight A gang, they were much more familiar with the subject of international criminals and kidnapping than they would have liked to be. But that wasn't something they were about to share with their classmates.

Rainbow turned to Laura. 'We would never have found Camilla if it hadn't been for you and Tariq. Is there any way that you can work a miracle and track down Miss Creswell?'

'There is one possibility . . . Camilla, when you gave Miss Creswell those hay-fever tablets, did you look at the label? Were they non-drowsy pills or were they the kind that put you to sleep?'

Camilla's brow wrinkled. 'I'm not sure. Do you think . . . ? Oh, no!'

'I suspect,' said Laura, 'that Miss Creswell is exactly where we expected her to be all along.'

SEVEN

The five children, by now firm friends, stood staring down at Miss Creswell, who was sleeping peacefully in the armchair in the cottage bedroom.

'But *how?*' whispered Rainbow. 'I don't understand. Where was she when we came looking for her? We searched everywhere.'

Laura put her finger to her lips and they tiptoed out and shut the door.

Once in the garden, everyone fired questions at her. How did she know the teacher would be there? Where had Miss Creswell been when they were looking for her? Where was she hiding?

'She wasn't hiding anywhere. She's been napping in the armchair all along.'

'Don't be ridiculous,' said Rainbow. 'Me, Adam and Nico went in and out of the room about five times and you and Tariq saw it too.'

'Yes, we did. But each of us assumed that she'd be in or on the bed. When she wasn't, we didn't think to look in the corner of the room beside the mirror.'

'I don't believe you,' Adam said. 'If she

was there, we would have seen her. I know we would have.'

'Not necessarily. My uncle used to be a detective and he told me that most people's brains can only take in four bits of visual information at a time – less if there are other distractions. When each of you walked into Miss Creswell's room, you expected to see her in or near the bed. When she wasn't, you were distracted by different things – her phone on the pillow and the fact it was dead, or the Beast of Bodmin roaring on the moor. The same happened when Tariq and I entered the cottage. We saw the reflection of the bed in the mirror and assumed that because the room is so tiny and three people had already checked it, it must be empty.'

Camilla broke in. 'That's fascinating and if we could ever tell anyone what happened I would nominate Laura for some kind of Detective of the Year Award. I'm so grateful to you, Laura – well, to all of you. I was convinced that I was going to die alone on the moors. But since I haven't, I'm going to jump in the shower before anyone sees me looking like I've been dragged through a bog by the Beast of Bodmin.'

'I'm next,' said Laura.

'And I'm after you,' said Tariq.

Adam looked out at the moors. The fog was dissolving and high in the sky was the first pink hint of dawn. 'Any chance of breakfast when we're done with all the scrubbing and cleaning? I don't know about the rest of you but I'm starving.'

And so it was that when Miss Creswell emerged from the cottage at 8.02 a.m., having woken with a start in the armchair, she saw something astounding. Nearly all of her class were washed, combed and dressed and tucking into a breakfast of banana nut muffins, coffee and fried egg rolls prepared by Jamie. The most startling thing was how happy they all looked. Camilla and Rainbow Brown, who had appeared to be mortal enemies on the way to Bodmin, were giggling over a shared joke. Even Laura Marlin's rather fearsome Siberian husky looked innocent.

'Apologies, everyone,' she said as she hurried up to them, trying to smooth her hair and straighten her creased clothes. 'I have no idea what happened. One minute

I was trying to phone the hospital and the next I appear to have dozed off. Are you all okay? Any problems last night?'

Camilla gave her a big smile. 'None worth mentioning. Apart from being frightened out of our minds by ghosts, getting lost in the fog and being terrorised by the Beast of Bodmin, we had a great time.'

Miss Creswell clutched her heart. 'You're joking?'

Laura laughed. 'Yes, she is. Camilla did the most amazing job of taking care of us and Jamie cooked the best food ever, and . . .'

'And Laura, Tariq, Adam and Rainbow were heroes,' finished Camilla.

Miss Creswell was amused. 'Goodness, you have been busy.'

She took a muffin and was biting into it thoughtfully when Mrs Archer's car pulled up at the gate. Out stepped the two teachers, followed by a smiling Phillip. Amy came next, clutching a selection of coloured pens in her good hand. She wanted everyone to sign the cast on her left arm.

Mr Gillbert laughed when he saw the picnickers in the garden. 'I can't believe I wasted a moment worrying about bringing you all to the moor. As I climbed in a hotel bed in Truro after we were finished at the hospital, I felt guilty that we'd left you to fend for yourselves on such a foggy and, frankly, spooky night. We did try to call, but Miss Creswell's phone kept going to voicemail. I expect there was no signal. Did you sleep all right in your tents?'

'I didn't,' declared Katie, who was the only one still in pyjamas. 'The Beast of Bodmin was making hideous roaring noises for hours. Me and Sammi were petrified. Adam said it was just someone playing a game, but –'

'Adam was trying to be kind and comfort you, but he was wrong about the game,' interrupted Kayla, much to everyone's surprise. 'I saw the cat you heard. He was just an ordinary black moggy, but he sounded as if he'd swallowed a tiger. Maybe he had. I stroked him and he was actually quite friendly.'

As she turned away, she winked at Laura and Tariq.

'There you go, Katie,' said Mrs Archer, sipping a mug of tea. 'Sometimes our imaginations play tricks on us, especially at night, but there's always a simple explanation for everything. Now why don't you and Sammi take the last couple of banana muffins to make up for the lack of sleep?'

It was Tariq who spotted the paw print. He and Laura were packing up their tents and rucksacks when he noticed it in the dark earth. It was nearly three times the size of his palm. He grinned. 'Who you think made this, Laura? Do you think it was Adam, playing one last prank on us?'

Laura squatted down to study it. 'No human being has made this. It's too perfect.

Look, here's another one. There's no way that these are the tracks of an "ordinary moggy," as Kayla put it. They belong to a large and possibly highly dangerous predator.'

The grin left Tariq's face. He glanced around as if he expected the beast to be crouching in the branches of the nearby apple tree. 'Maybe they're old prints. I mean, we haven't had rain for at least two weeks so the chances are they were made before that. And maybe they don't belong to a cat. Perhaps Mr Gillbert's friends own a Great Dane or something.'

'Only a cat could have made these. You can tell because a cat's toe prints are shaped like tear drops and their palm makes three little hollows in the sand.

But these were made in the early hours of this morning, at around the same time I spilled my water bottle. It might even have happened while Adam and Rainbow were telling us that Camilla and Miss Creswell were missing.'

'And yet we didn't see it.'

'We didn't see it.'

'What about Skye? Wouldn't he have seen it?'

Laura shrugged. 'Perhaps he did. He was very agitated, but I thought it was to do with the roaring on the moors.'

'Hey, guys, everyone's getting on the bus,' called Adam from the garden gate. 'Are you coming home to St Ives or are you going to stay here with the Beast of Bodmin?'

Laura laughed. 'We're coming.'

Tariq slung his rucksack over his shoulder. 'What about the others – are we going to tell them?'

Laura used the toe of her boot to erase the paw. 'No, we're not. If it is a real panther, chances are that it's escaped from some awful zoo or circus. As far as I'm concerned, it's earned the right to be free. Every good detective knows that some mysteries are better left unsolved.'

**Collect all of
Lauren St John's books:**

The Laura Marlin Mysteries

DEAD MAN'S COVE

~ ~

KIDNAP IN THE CARIBBEAN

~ ~

KENTUCKY THRILLER

~ ~

RENDEZVOUS IN RUSSIA

The White Giraffe Quartet

The White Giraffe

Dolphin Song

The Last Leopard

The Elephant's Tale

The One Dollar Horse Trilogy

THE ONE DOLLAR HORSE

RACE THE WIND

FIRE STORM

the
orion star

★ ★ ★

CALLING ALL GROWN-UPS!
Sign up for **the orion star** newsletter to
hear about your favourite authors and exclusive
competitions, plus details of how children
can join our 'Story Stars' review panel.

Sign up at:

www.orionbooks.co.uk/orionstar

Follow us 🐦 @the_orionstar
Find us 📘 facebook.com/TheOrionStar

WORLD BOOK DAY *fest*

6 MARCH 2014

Want to **READ** more?

Visit your LOCAL BOOKSHOP

- Get some great recommendations for what to read next

- Meet your favourite authors & illustrators at brilliant events

- Discover books you never even knew existed!

WWW.BOOKSELLERS.ORG.UK/ BOOKSHOPSEARCH

Join your LOCAL LIBRARY

You can browse and borrow from a HUGE selection of books and get recommendations of what to read next from expert librarians—all for FREE! You can also discover libraries' wonderful children's and family reading activities.

WWW.FINDALIBRARY.CO.UK

GET ONLINE!

Visit **WWW.WORLDBOOKDAY.COM** to discover a whole *new* world of books!

- Downloads and activities
- Cool games, trailers and videos
- Author events in your area
- News, competitions and new books —all in a **FREE** monthly email